For my dream-come-true family,
Jason, Justin, Miles, and Paris
—A.K.R.

For all the daydreamers and believers
—B.B.

Text copyright © 2017 by Amy Krouse Rosenthal
Jacket art and interior illustrations copyright © 2017 by Brigette Barrager

Visit us on the Web! randomhousekids.com

Educators and librarians, for a variety of teaching tools,
visit us at RHTeachersLibrarians.com

Library of Congress Cataloging-in-Publication Data is available upon request.
ISBN 978-1-101-93659-7 (trade) — ISBN 978-1-101-93660-3 (lib. bdg.) —
ISBN 978-1-101-93661-0 (ebook)

MANUFACTURED IN CHINA
10 9 8 7
First Edition

Uni the UNICORN and the Dream Come True

Avery book

Amy Krouse Rosenthal

illustrated by Brigette Barrager

RANDOM HOUSE NEW YORK

*I*t had been raining and raining and raining in the land of unicorns.

Which meant there hadn't been any sunshine
(for what seemed like forever).

Which meant there hadn't been any rainbows
(for what seemed like forever).

Which meant there hadn't been any magic
(for what seemed like forever).

Because remember,
there are only three ways unicorns can get
their strength and magic:

From the golden sun.
From magnificent rainbows.
From the sparkle of believing.

Luckily, there was a bright ray of hope
from the one unicorn who believed
that little girls were REAL.

And this is why Uni, and only Uni, was as strong
and magical as ever.

But Uni was very concerned about all the other unicorns.

Meanwhile, somewhere far away (but not *that* far away), a little girl watched the rain from her window.

Somehow she knew she was desperately needed in the land of unicorns.

(She was smart that way.)

The more it poured, the more certain she was.

The harder it rained, the harder Uni believed.

The longer it stormed, the more they longed to finally be together.

All of a sudden, they both heard thunder.

CLAP

CLAP!

They both saw lightning.

ZAP

ZAP!

They closed their eyes tight
and wished the same wish with all their might.

Then everything went white and quiet.

"It's really you!"
the little girl shouted.

"You're really REAL!"
(Though Uni had never once doubted.)

They could have laughed and hugged for hours,
but there was no time to waste.

They ran quickly through the meadow!

They stopped to help some forest creatures in need.

And together, they lifted spirits.

At last, they discovered the unicorns huddled under a large tree.

And the unicorns discovered what Uni had known all along.

"It's true! You knew!
Little girls are REAL!"

Believing and befriending, each and every unicorn became, once again, sparkly, strong, and magical.

As for the endless rain, Uni alone hadn't been able to wish it away.

But TOGETHER, could the unicorns make such a wish come true?

Could they ever!

After what seemed like forever, the rain stopped.
The clouds parted. And the golden sun appeared.

Uni and the little girl twirled and twirled.

What they didn't know, but would marvel at soon enough . . . was that the sun would bring not ONE but TWO *extra*-magnificent rainbows!

And since rainbows are the bridge between Here and There, a double rainbow meant that not only could the little girl return home, but there was a place for one more.

Of course of course of course
you know who she chose.

She couldn't wait
for her family and friends
to finally meet
Uni the unicorn.